The Evelyn R. Flug Children's Library
PITKIN COUNTY LIBRARY
1 13 0001895365
W9-DGN-268
EASY READER B763 BRIDWELL
Bridwell, Norman. 10.25
Clifford makes a friend
WITHDRAWN
120 NORTH MILL STREET • ASPEN, COLORADO 81611

NORMAN BRIDWELL

Clifford® Makes a Friend

Hello Reader! — Level 1

SCHOLASTIC INC. Cartwheel BOOKS®
New York Toronto London Auckland Sydney

The boy sees the dog.

The dog sees the boy.

The boy runs.

The dog runs.

The boy jumps.

The dog jumps.

The boy and the dog
spin and spin and spin.

The boy makes a face.

The dog makes a face.

The boy laughs.

The dog licks the boy.
He likes boys who laugh.

The boy does a cartwheel.

So does the dog.

They are friends.

• Word List •

a	face	runs
and	friends	sees
are	he	so
boy	jumps	spin
boys	laughs	the
cartwheel	licks	they
does	likes	who
dog	makes